129   9⁰⁰

D1174264

DESPERATE CHARACTERS

ALSO BY NICHOLAS CHRISTOPHER

Desperate Characters

A Novella in Verse
& other poems

Nicholas Christopher

VIKING

VIKING
Published by the Penguin Group
Viking Penguin Inc., 40 West 23rd Street, New York, New York 10010, U.S.A.
Penguin Books Ltd, 27 Wrights Lane, London W8 5TZ, England
Penguin Books Australia Ltd, Ringwood, Victoria, Australia
Penguin Books Canada Ltd, 2801 John Street, Markham,
Ontario, Canada L3R 1B4
Penguin Books (N.Z.) Ltd, 182–190 Wairau Road, Auckland 10, New Zealand

Penguin Books Ltd, Registered Offices:
Harmondsworth, Middlesex, England

First published in 1988 by Viking Penguin Inc.
Published simultaneously in Canada

1 2 3 4 5 6 7 8 9 10

Copyright © Nicholas Christopher, 1988
All rights reserved

Some of the poems in this collection first appeared in magazines as follows:

"Krazy Kat" as "Desperate Character" and
"Green Animals" in *The New Yorker*;
"Collecting Stamps in Port-Au-Prince" in *The Yale Review*;
"Voyeur" and "The Hottest Night of the Year" in *Shenandoah*;
"Elegy for My Grandmother" in *The Missouri Review*;
"Circe Revisited" and "Miranda in Reno" in *The New Republic*;
"Christmas, 1956" and "Circe in Love" in *The Nation*;
and "Map" in *Southwest Review*.

Grateful acknowledgment is made for permission to reprint an excerpt from
The Great Wall of China by Franz Kafka, translated by Willa and
Edwin Muir. Copyright 1936, 1937 by Heinrich Mercy Sohn, Prague.
Copyright 1946 and renewed 1974 by Schocken Books, Inc.
Reprinted by permission of the publisher.

LIBRARY OF CONGRESS CATALOGING IN PUBLICATION DATA
Christopher, Nicholas.
Desperate characters & other poems.
I. Title. II. Title: Desperate characters and other poems.
PS3553.H754D47 1988   811'.54   87–40567
ISBN 0–670–82399–6

Printed in the United States of America by
Arcata Graphics, Fairfield, Pennsylvania
Set in Bodoni
Designed by Francesca Belanger

Without limiting the rights under copyright reserved above,
no part of this publication may be reproduced, stored in or introduced
into a retrieval system, or transmitted, in any form or by any means
(electronic, mechanical, photocopying, recording or otherwise),
without the prior written permission of both the copyright
owner and the above publisher of this book.

In memory of Howard Moss
and for Constance

Leopards break into the temple and drink the sacrificial chalices dry; this occurs repeatedly, again and again: finally it can be reckoned upon beforehand and becomes a part of the ceremony.

—FRANK KAFKA

Acknowledgments

I am most grateful to The National Endowment for the Arts, The New York Foundation for the Arts, and the trustees of the Amy Lowell Poetry Travelling Scholarship for their generous support while I was writing this book.

And for their kind assistance, I wish to thank Anthony Hecht and Melanie Jackson, and to express special thanks and appreciation to my editor, Amanda Vaill.

Contents

I
....

Desperate Characters

Here you are in Hollywood
on an empty stomach in an unlit room.
A blonde wearing a sombrero
and fur-lined slippers
has just told you your fortune
by the open window
overlooking the pepper trees.
She said someone you once crossed
is coming back into your life,
bringing pain and destruction;
a woman with steel suitcases
stamped BEDLAM in red.
You think of the odd enemies
you've made in strange cities,
and of the friends who
from time to time reassemble
on the periphery of your life
in changing formations.
Then you gaze out past
the trees to a vacant lot
bricked in sunlight—
clear amber bars laid in neatly
around a garden of tin cans and weeds.
Up in the hills, blue smoke
sweet as incense
is swirling from the brushfires.
People in white capes and hoods
are ringing bells and keening.
Last night at a party
you met a pair of female
impersonators speaking in tongues.
After relating joyous news

from the holy land,
they ate mushrooms
and waded into the swimming pool
howling like coyotes.
Through a glass door you watched
the surf break in the distance
while someone told you confidentially
that what's really important
is the way time passes in dreams
when you're not dreaming.
(Later, you dreamt of a dead man
in Honolulu being lowered
into a grave full of
freshly cut flowers.)
Another guest was a man
with a ring on every finger
who announced that he'd been married
many times to death.
Your hostess was a teenage widow,
heiress to a junkyard magnate,
an octogenarian named Belinsky
with a taste for schoolgirls
and a famous collection
of gold fruit pitted with gems,
including six miniature
pineapples more valuable
than the Tsar's Fabergé eggs.
It was the widow Belinsky
who introduced you to a mute
couple who have crossed America
four times on foot,
scouring the great continent
in search of Thomas Jefferson's ghost,
last seen (they said) sticking up
a savings & loan in Denver,
now rumored to be hiding out in L.A.
But the mediums in town

have never even heard of Jefferson;
your naked fortune-teller,
for example, her sombrero aslant,
her eyes twinkling madly
in the darkness, insists that
"from Denver he would hightail it
south into the desert,
where entire cities of ghosts
sprawl for miles.
To New Mexico . . ."

On the roof in a red
beach-chair, you fry
all afternoon like a fish.
The cement floor is painted pink,
the potted palms are dusty.
The wall tiles, hourglass-shaped,
are mortared in black.
You're alone for a few hours
with a radio and a cooler of beer.
Jets are streaking by,
the sun glinting on their wings.
On a nearby balcony
two parrots are squabbling.
A woman in a wheelchair
is watering a leafless tree.
Her nurse is scanning the neighboring
apartments with binoculars.
The honeysuckle is choking you.
Are you Chuang Tzu's butterfly,
dreaming of yourself as a man?
Flying over the Mississippi
you grew queasy; skimming the Rockies
you felt your lungs tighten.
You sipped tequila, trying

to sidestep the vague
but powerful uneasiness propelling
you 3000 miles west.
And now you learn that some woman
bent on violence is seeking you
out for reasons unknown.
In New York she would never
find you, but in this city
of crazies, of low houses
and parched open spaces
and informers a dime a dozen,
she'll have no trouble
tracking you down.
But who is she?
Your friend in the sombrero
is soaking in a tub of ice water—
you yourself emptied the three
trays of ice cubes from the freezer
onto her glistening body
while she whistled through pale
lips, her eyes half-lidded.
What is the future but a web
of lies waiting to be rewoven,
and what is the soothsayer
if not a liar
waiting to be found out?
Emperors like Claudius and Otho
learned this too late
and paid heavily for their ignorance.
But you are no emperor
and you should stop drinking
so much in this heat.
Rather, try to peel away
the ether-laden layers
of this tight sky until
you survey its white onion core,
bulb-shaped, dimly lit, enfolding

the promise of another city
where the architects are saints
and the carpenters angels.
Only this morning, downtown,
you glimpsed a trio of workmen
in white coveralls on a scaffold
forty stories high
waving their hats to a troupe
of Japanese dancers
in the park below;
imagine the possibilities
if such men were to construct,
not another insurance company tower
with black mirrored windows,
but a great hall of aqueous marble—
maybe twenty miles square—
with hundreds of tiers
and a dozen revolving stages
each supporting a dance company
swimming in blue light
to the strains of an orchestra
with (for starters) 3000 violins,
1000 cellos, 200 timpani
and 500 flutes; and imagine
this hall as a mere corner
of a single plaza tucked away
in our vast hypothetical city.
Of course these same workmen
might well scorn your lofty
blueprint, all that *ars gratia
artis* mumbo-jumbo, as nothing
more than a pipe dream
under a 90-degree sun—
but what is that to you?
And what would Jefferson—
no mean architect himself—
have said to all of this?

No, you're raving again.
You've been raving ever since
you arrived in this town
and sombrero-cum-slippers,
in a gauzy Chinese robe
and red heels, a pearl-handled
.38 strapped to her shoulder,
picked you up at the airport
in a gray limo with Hawaiian plates
and played you a tape-recorded
greeting from some people
you thought were dead.
"No, it's not them," she smiled.
"These are other strangers . . ."

Speaking of which, as the night
slides in in darkening blue
sheets, and the surrounding
streets are suddenly revealed
to be lacquered black, with Day Glo
dragons stenciled over intersections,
a stranger dressed in a familiar
suit—the one you've worn
to all your relatives' funerals—
enters the courtyard below
clicking a silver cane,
leading a black dog on a short leash,
and even from six stories up
you can see the stranger's
white moustache twitching,
his slit eyes unblinking:
he has some news for you,
if only you invite him up.
Your hostess, who is also
your bodyguard (she straps on her

revolver again under a pink kimono)
tells you to start calling her
Stella—her third name
in as many days,
which is okay with you.
Then she sets out a pot of espresso
and a bottle of brandy,
but the stranger will suffer
no amenities; he gets
right down to business.
And you hope his "news"
does not concern this crazy woman
who is supposedly tracking you down—
could he be her agent?
Suddenly you're grateful for
that rod Stella is packing.
But, no, he's come about
Jefferson's ghost!
A theosophist and undercover cop,
with credentials a foot long,
he's flown up from Santa Fe
hot on the trail of that mute couple
you met recently at
the widow Belinsky's party.
(At the mention of New Mexico
Stella casts you a long look,
as if to say, I told you so.)
It seems those two are charlatans,
Romanian opera singers on the lam,
who have eluded the bunko
squads of a dozen cities
while preying on patriotic
societies who pay handsomely
for a half hour
of questions & answers
with our third President.
"Singers? You mean they can talk?"

"When it suits them," he replies darkly.
"I'm questioning everyone
  they've had contact with
  here in L.A.
  All else aside, it appears
  they stole the 24-karat Belinsky
  pineapples the other night.
  So if you run into them again,
  give me a call."
He hands you his card
  and heads for the door
  and you notice that he carries
  a paintbrush and a cluster
  of scallions in his back pocket.
  The card reads: Z. ZIMMER/TOPEKA.
"And by the way," he whispers
  when you hand him his cane,
"have you heard there's a woman
  coming after you?
  Her last known address,
  many years ago,
  was a crazyhouse in Florida—
  then you do know,
  I can see it in your eyes.
  Keep a sharp lookout,
  word is she's armed and dangerous.
  And she wears a necklace
  strung with snake bones."
Before you can squeeze
  any more details out of him,
  he's gone, the steel taps
  on his boots throwing off sparks
  on the courtyard stones,
  and his black dog,
  tethered to a lamppost,
  kicking up a fearful racket
  when his master reappears.

In the kitchen, Stella stands
naked in her other slippers—
clear plastic with green pom-poms—
tossing a jalapeño omelette
and singing along to the radio.
She has inserted red
light bulbs into all the lamps
in the living room,
so when you sit down again,
your head racing,
you feel as if you are
underwater in hell.
Outside, blue snakes are tangling
in midair, and the wind
is whistling hard
through the pepper trees.
As stormclouds gather,
it sounds as if the sky
is crisscrossed with runaway trains.

For several days you sleep badly.
Stella says you have great sex
together—but don't you ever
want to go out anymore?
Maybe just to the beach . . .
You go to the beach,
she in a chauffeur's cap
behind the wheel of the gray limo
and you in the rear seat,
Arctic air gushing over you
from the air-conditioning vents
as you gaze through the tinted
window at the shadow-play
the sun is casting on the freeway—
ghosts flitting through the glare—

and in your ears the tires
on the scalding pavement
begin to whine with progressions
of viola and violin, faster
and more demented by the second.
Furies are streaming in your wake,
and when Stella offers
you a nip of tequila
from her pocket flask,
you take it gladly—
and you keep the flask.
After finding a niche
in the ivory dunes,
you spread a blanket
and she strips and falls asleep
with her revolver wrapped up
in the towel under her head.
Around her nipples the areolae
erupt in dark granules.
Her thighs gleam with oil.
Her purple toenails glimmer
with promise, like amethysts.
Four days have passed
and she is still calling herself Stella.
How would you describe her, really?
Eyes gray, hair bleached
(from her mons, jet-black,
it's clear she's no blonde),
a mole on her cheek
worthy of the coquettes in Molière;
legs long, breasts full,
and an abdomen like a washboard.
She gets by in Spanish and Japanese
and says she used to work for
Pinkerton's—just like Sam Spade.
Her laconic conversation
is sprinkled with phrases like

"opaque depths of reason"
  & "deadpan anguish"
  & "perverse southpaw diligence."
One morning you caught her off-guard,
at ease in the Jacuzzi,
scented with violet powders,
and she told you
one of her recurrent dreams:
a great golden condor
is gliding in the wind currents
miles above the *Sierra Pinta*
in the Baja, traveling
a series of concentric circles
to a point directly above her,
and as he hovers there,
gilded by the desert sun,
she hears a commotion
in the underbrush—
men greased with body-paint,
their hair thick with ashes,
emerge howling, blowing whistles
and clattering pots & pans.
Several, with bloodstained lips,
carry machetes in their teeth.
She tries to run away,
but instead begins ascending
slowly on the wind,
along a spiraling vortex,
and when she reaches the condor,
falling into the centrifugal
pull of his orbit
high in the clear air,
he locks his talons around her
wrists and pulls her to his breast,
her hips wriggling and legs shuddering
as his enormous wings beat
harder and harder,

and they climb up beyond
the bare mountain peaks,
miles above the icy clouds,
and just as she catches sight
of the Pacific far to the west,
blue and hazy and abstract,
he releases her
and she wakes up falling,
screaming for help
at the top of her lungs.
"Like Leda," you said.
unable to picture Stella,
such a cool customer,
ever screaming for help.
But Stella had never heard of
Leda or her swan,
and dipping her head
under the Jacuzzi's fast jet,
the blonde hair waterfalling,
she looked that morning
much as she does now
lifting herself from the surf
with exaggerated slowness
while you gaze at her from shore.

That night you learn about
Stella's relationship with Rocco,
a.k.a. Rocco the Human Cannonball,
who clearly doesn't have a Ledaean bent.
With an iron grip—
a paw like a polar bear's—
he introduces himself as Stella's ex,
though they've never been married.
Your own temporary relations
with her seem of no interest

to him . . . he's overflowing
with his own problems.
As the red light bulbs radiate
off his shaved head
(tattooed above the right ear
with a naked girl riding a sea horse),
he rumbles his litany of grievances.
He's with a circus, and he's suing
the management for negligence.
You tune out of the conversation
(while Stella listens
sympathetically, replenishing
his shot glass with tequila)
and try to take stock
of what exactly you're doing
in this town after so many days.
Your "business," such as it was,
the last legal imbroglio
in a messy divorce case in Tijuana,
was concluded weeks ago,
and after a brief detour
to Las Vegas, you came into L.A.
for a few days' R&R,
"to cool out," as someone advised
you at Lake Tahoe over martinis—
a dozen hits of cocaine lined up
on the glass bar like runways
and a blizzard raging in your head—
the same nightclub drifter
(white tux/red wig/cowboy boots)
who contacted Stella and arranged
your accommodations in Tinsel Town.
Things got complicated
because you made a killing
at the roulette wheel,
putting everything on black
twelve times running,

so suddenly you had more
enemies in the world
than your ex-wife and her lawyer—
mob guys, casino bigshots,
and their stooge in the sheriff's
office, didn't like anybody
(especially a hopped-up greenhorn
who bragged that he had
"broken the banks
at Deauville and Biarritz")
to get that lucky;
they wanted to ask you
a few routine questions,
to check you out, but you skipped
town and lost most of the cash
in an all-night poker game
on the express train to Reno.
For sixteen hours you were
a millionaire, as every American
should be once in his life,
and now you've got enough
left to pay alimony
and idle with the likes
of Stella for a year or so—
that is, if the likes of Stella
will have you.
Then it hits you:
maybe Z. Zimmer, of Topeka,
was also a mob guy—
maybe the drifter at Tahoe, too,
and even Stella and Rocco.
What if this crazy woman
they keep warning you about
is just a ruse to put you off
your guard for a while?
You study Rocco with new interest
through the smoke of your cigar

as he stops railing about the circus
lawyers and, sitting back heavily,
asks Stella to put some
Charlie Parker on the stereo.
He's partial to the saxophone's
melancholy runs, the minor
keys that reconnect memories
of better times, of lingering
desires and the close spaces
they inhabit like hothouse flowers.
Rocco is a big man
with a big tired heart.
"Remember, Stella, the time
you had that job in San Diego
watching over the Arab sheik
and his three wives
and we grabbed a few hours
at the aquarium with wife #2?"
Stella remembers it all,
in intricate detail:
Rocco's fascination with the giant
octopus from the Malay peninsula,
and the Beluga whales,
white as Moby-Dick,
mating in a black tank,
and the barracudas at feeding time,
and above all the Bedouin
princess in traditional white
robes hemmed with purple lace
(herself an attraction to
the suburban crowd)
who dumbfounded Rocco
with her utter ignorance of marine life.
"Because she had never left the desert . . ."
Penguins, on stinking hillocks,
shitting openly in their pool,
and open-sea turtles motoring

their enormous bulks,
and sea horses, suspended with frozen eyes,
and the mako sharks butting
the three-inch glass and showing
their keyboards of razor teeth
that play only one song:
all of this was strange to her,
and they would have brought her
back for more, but the other
wives were jealous,
and the sheik forbade it.
Stella turns up the *Savoy Sessions*
as Parker and Davis duel over
Curly Russell's throbbing bass,
and Rocco, beaming over
his aquarium recollections
and clearly talked-out,
downs a last tequila.
He watches Stella glide
into the kitchen, and then
turns his small eyes on you.
"That sheik was worth
$200 million—can you imagine?—
and he had three more wives
and twenty-two kids back home.
Stella and I had a kid,"
he adds, "adopted by mail,
in Indonesia. You know,
we'd send dough every month.
But she died of malaria."

On Saturday Stella takes you
on a whirlwind tour
of the nightspots she favors:
a dive where a woman

in a leopard skin snatches
coins from the air with a lariat;
and a huge cavern
four stories underground
where midgets in loincloths
wrestle in a mock-lagoon;
and a private club on a barge
moored off Redondo Beach
where girls wearing nothing
but skullcaps and ribbons
dance with rubber cobras
under a pink waterfall.
In the wee hours you visit
Stella's dealer, to score some hashish.
Opiated stuff, from Morocco:
the brick from which he cuts
you six grams is lettered
in yellow, with Arabic characters.
Stella fills her hookah
with crème de menthe
and you drive up to the hills
overlooking the city,
and with the radio turned on low,
you pull hard on the clear tube
and the green liquid bubbles
while the smoke pours
into your lungs, expands,
and sets off a distant
drumming in your ears.
The far provinces of your brain
light up, topaz and ruby,
like the twinkling networks
of Los Angeles stretching
as far as you can see
(not really a city,
as you know the term,
but a crazy quilt of suburbs),

from Catalina to San Bernardino—
and Stella, truly clairvoyant,
suddenly pipes into your thoughts,
exhaling blue haloes with a sigh:
"You see the problem before you—
there's no center to this place.
No Times Square, no Loop
or Bourbon Street—and that's why
everyone here is uncentered too.
These streets flow nowhere.
These buildings are empty.
Think of it as a ghost town."
So you've come full circle
(or as Stella would say,
"full figure-eight—
the sign for infinity"),
and now she's coughing up
the theories of those Romanian
opera singers (posing as mutes)
who are so sure
Jefferson's ghost is holed up
in the City of the Angels.
"Greater L.A. is 5000 square miles,"
she continues, "and if you transplanted
it to the moon for a few days—
facing the sun, of course—
no one here would notice . . ."
Meanwhile, you're busy calculating:
when Jefferson was President
California was a Spanish colony
administered from Mexico;
not until twenty-four years
after his death, in 1850,
did it join the Union,
the 31st State,
during the Polk Administration.
You learn all this the next

morning at one of the remoter
branches of the public library,
a little adobe building
with a terra-cotta roof
tucked into a triangle of palm
trees on a dead-end street
called Thomas Paine Lane.
Stella, insisting you're not safe
in crowded places,
has brought you by a circuitous
route, past dusty orange
groves and scrap-metal yards
and a shantytown of cardboard
lean-tos and tattered tents,
and then through a maze
of sleepy residential streets
with solid boxy houses and big cars
parked under black trees.
Outside the library,
beside a weathered cannon
and a dozen cannonballs soldered
into a pyramid,
the flag is flying at half-staff
on a 200-foot pole.
Someone has died, but even the librarian
can't say who it is.
You glance at the calendar,
and by some coincidence,
it's July 4th—
the day Jefferson died.
But that can't be!
No public buildings would be open.
The librarian shrugs again
and disappears into the stacks.
Before you leave the reference
books a few minutes later
and return to Stella

chain-smoking in the limo
with the air-conditioner purring,
you also discover that Jefferson
was the first President seriously
interested in the western USA,
that he in fact dreamt up
the Lewis & Clark expedition
and negotiated the Louisiana Purchase.
In the same history of California,
many chapters later, your eye
catches on an obscure footnote:
CHOP SUEY: from the Cantonese
shap sui ("odds & ends"),
invented San Francisco ca. 1900
by the Chinese laborers who built
the railroads at 2¢ an hour—
the first of our many fast foods,
that Mulligan stew of the Golden West,
concocted half a century
before the burger & fries
and half a century after statehood!
Chronologically, at least, chop suey
lies at the center of something.

The trip to the library
assumes far greater importance
for what transpires *afterwards*.
If Stella didn't choose
that particular hideaway branch,
you would not cross paths with Z. Zimmer
for the second time that week,
under even more peculiar circumstances.
First, though, you realize
you have forgotten your sunglasses
at the library, and despite Stella's

determined efforts to retrace
your path through the maze
of shady blocks,
it takes a half hour
to find that dead-end street
named after the great radical
and—lo!—instead of a library
there in the wedge of palms
a silver velodrome has materialized,
with concession stands
and parking lots,
and cyclists from around the country
competing in the blazing heat.
There is no cannon,
and no soldered cannonballs—
only the flagpole is the same,
but the flag is run up
all the way, fluttering fast.
And there are fireworks going off
suddenly in every direction:
ash-cans and cherry bombs,
rockets and Roman candles.
It *is* the 4th of July!
Maybe you and Stella should not
have smoked so much hash
last night in the Hollywood Hills.
And then reefer in cinnamon
papers while you frolicked
in the Jacuzzi at dawn.
But never mind.
Z. Zimmer, posing as a blind man,
in dark glasses, his black
dog leading him, is hobbling out
of the shantytown as you pass by
on the way back into town.
Stella pulls over and you watch
a cop help him cross the street,

and then Zimmer comes right up
to the limo and leans in
the window, grinning.
This time he has a small flashlight
and a sprig of coriander
in his handkerchief pocket.
"I just missed them," he mutters,
"by a few hours.
The opera singers, I mean.
It seems the diva set up as a gypsy
there among the transients.
She was reading palms
in a corrugated shack.
Telling those folks their *for*-tunes,"
he chuckles, "in some weird lingo.
See, I've learned that before
she went in for singing
over in Bucharest
she had a good racket going.
People would come to her studio
to rub elbows with dead kings & queens.
Napoleon, Charlemagne, Isabella—
you name it—she'd conjure up
the spirit on demand for the suckers.
That's where all this hocus-pocus
about Jefferson comes in—
she just switched continents.
Before I forget, I believe
these are yours," he smiles,
removing the shades
and handing them to you.
"Meet me on Friday night
at ten o'clock on the beach
at San Pedro, down the coast—
by the old lighthouse.
You might find it interesting.
In fact, there's something

in it for you—
both of you," he winks,
and Stella pales slightly.
"That little number who's been
on your tail—maybe we can
straighten all that out.
Until then . . ."
Slapping the shantytown dust
from his shoulders like dandruff,
he flags down a cab,
scoops the dog up in his arms,
and is gone.
And it's true!
They are the sunglasses you lost
at the phantom library.

On the roof under the stars
Stella reveals her nakedness
to you, as if for the first time.
It's very late.
Even in east Los Angeles
the fireworks have died down.
Fast purple clouds are streaming
across the mountains,
and from the cassette player
soft Egyptian music,
bells and drums and flutes,
is wafting over you.
You stretch out on the beach-chair
while Stella nooses a flashlight
to the clothesline,
the hard white beam boring
through the blackness
like a spotlight
as she drops her robe

and begins to dart in and out
of the shadows, gyrating
so that the light freezes
her at odd angles—
a breast in profile,
a hip, an outstretched hand,
her pelvis beaded with sweat
and her face wide-eyed
and white, like a mask.
And then, with a cry,
when the music crescendoes,
she flings herself on top
of you, breathing fast,
and bites your shoulder so hard
that you scream and flip her
over, your hand groping
between her legs,
your mouth glued to her throat
as she hisses in your ear
and digs her nails
into your back.

Meditating on a pair of swallows
as they build a nest in the eaves
of the gutted bank across
the street, you sip
mint tea through a straw.
At the turn of the century
that Gothic monolith
was full of gold bars,
the melted veins
of the great desert mountains.
Now the dank vaults are ankle-deep
in pigeon shit and ashes.
Stella cannibalized one of

the old teller's cages
and transformed it
into a three-dimensional trellis
covered with morning glories
which she keeps on the balcony.
The brass slot through which thousands
of bills of all denominations
slid daily is now bursting
forth a profusion of violets.
Stella refers to this floral
display as "the aviary"
because every day at dawn
a pair of songbirds descends
from the egg-blue sky,
perches among the blossoms
and performs duets while she bathes.
You recall something Rocco said
about the Arab princess
as you survey the ruins
of the San Rafael National Bank
with infrared binoculars—
the frescoes of dark angels
with longbows, and zaftig
madonnas on horseback,
and cherubs romping in a brook;
and the shattered marble counters,
splintered chandeliers, and oak benches
where mortgagors and creditors
waited for a hearing from
one of the dozen assistant
managers in airless cubicles—
Rocco said: "That woman's hands
had never touched a dollar bill,
yet she was worth thirty,
maybe forty million liquid.
It's like people who believe
in God," he nodded, "or people

in love: they don't even
have to think about it.
But people with nothing always
have plenty to think about."
And Stella, massaging his massive
shoulders from behind,
winked at you with a sad smile.

Leaving a Chinese restaurant
on a deserted street at 2 A.M.,
you hear a shot ring out
and a peal of laughter,
and then a white sedan screeches
around the corner on two wheels,
burning rubber on the hot tar.
Stella pushes you to the ground,
whips out her .38
and crouches behind a parked car,
only her eyes moving.
You wonder if you've stumbled
onto a movie set.
"Maybe it was a backfire,"
you suggest, a bag
of egg rolls and chop suey
crushed between your chest
and the sidewalk—
but Stella will have none of it.
"It's her," she replies,
scanning the caged storefronts
and chewing the wad of gum
in her molars back to life.
"The one with the steel suitcases.
The crazy.
Well, now she's found you."

Even the moon has begun
to look hot
through the curtains of mist.
Like a coin retrieved
from a furnace
before it can melt.
Yet outside of the limo,
Stella maintains an aversion
to air conditioners.
She prefers to bucket ice
into her bath, and to surround
her oval bed with a dozen
high-powered table fans
that whir you both into
a troubled sleep—
as if you're taking off
in one of those prewar Clippers,
off a boiling sea,
with Howard Hughes at the throttle.
Except that he ejects immediately,
leaving all twelve propellers
on automatic pilot,
speeding you into your nightmares
at the red altitudes
while he glides down like Daedalus,
natty in his white uniform,
a starlet under each wax wing
singing his favorite aria
from Puccini . . . and then he takes
off again in another plane,
over and over again,
forever leaving
the earth behind in a rush
of foam and smoke and thunder—
and you pray eternity
will treat you so kindly.

Even if you are plugged
from a moving car,
clutching a bag of chop suey,
with bitter laughter echoing
in your ears.
But the images that snap
the tenuous threads of your sleep
and bring you padding from bed
at all hours, through the fans,
over the cool Mexican tiles
for a shot of tequila
in the kitchen,
are usually far more mundane.
Centering around your lust.
Stella sleeps in the buff,
of course, her breasts pushing up—
perfectly formed as stone—
against the peach sheets,
her arms tossed back,
the underarms jasmine-scented,
and her fingers poised (upside-
down) on the rosewood headboard
as if over a Steinway,
playing chromatic scales
in the cell of *her* dreams.
From down the dark hallway
in the middle of the night
it's as if she's thousands
of miles away—
you feel lonely and *unprotected*,
and not because of the revolver
under her pillow.
The tequila doesn't help.
But when you stumble on
a thin blue photo album
in the cupboard atop the refrigerator
(behind the shot glasses),

it's as if you've discovered
a Gutenberg Bible.
Here is Stella's childhood
in the Florida Keys,
on a houseboat painted aquamarine,
her bearded father laughing
as he lifts her from the sea
in a fishing net;
and her marriage to a Cuban
nightclub singer who was executed
gangland-style for double-crossing
a cocaine kingpin in Nassau;
and her sister taking holy
orders in Lucerne
while Stella stands solemnly
to one side in a fur parka;
and Stella and Rocco
on a roller coaster
in Long Beach with long-stemmed
roses in their teeth;
and Stella—a recent shot—
attending a funeral in Honolulu,
veiled in white,
tossing a bouquet of freesia
into an open grave;
and Stella alone on her balcony,
naked from the breasts up,
a timer-delayed self-portrait
taken on an overcast morning;
her gray irises darkly
furled around the edges,
her pupils circular black islands—
seen aerially—around which
gray waves are breaking;
and playing over her tense
lips, white at the corners,
the smile of a drowning woman.

Inked in red at the base
of this photograph is a date
which stops the breath
in your throat—
for it lies in the future,
the coming Friday, in fact,
the day Z. Zimmer has invited you
to a rendezvous at San Pedro.
Unless of course
there is some mistake . . .

Once, at the end of your
rope (another rope) in Paris,
watching snow slant over the green
rooftops into the river,
you took a taxi out
to Versailles and walked
the Sun King's icy maze
and prayed that the blood
flying through the corridors
of your heart—
vast and intricate
as the palace rising before you
in the dirty fog—
might never freeze.
At that moment you realized
that just when the business
of suffering seems to be ending,
it is really only just beginning.
Thomas Jefferson, American
minister to France in 1789,
once wandered that same maze
reading the Emperor Marcus Aurelius,
who penned his *Meditations*
on the swampy islands

of the Danube while waging
a futile campaign against the barbarians
and receiving constant reports
of the plagues, floods and rebellions
that were eating away
at his Empire; he wrote:
"I, who have never
willfully pained another,
have no business
to pain myself."
Like many other Americans,
the minister took no solace
in this advice.
Like you, who left the European
capital in dead of night,
the brown clouds forked lividly
by electrical storms,
to fly west, to the New World,
the frontier spoiling under its red sky,
to the Pacific
where the light dies,
where how many million
American hands, bloodied
in ravaging the Indian's continent,
the blood caked hard
in creased palms,
were dipped into the gray,
darkly breaking waves,
around a black center.
Like Stella's eyes in that picture.
You glimpsed them back then
while leaving Paris, before
Stella was even the shadow
of a shadow for you,
and they have come back
to haunt you in moments
of guilt and desperation.

So that it was many years
before you got up the nerve,
through a failure of nerve,
to travel west again.
Drowning. Black with pain.
And that's the real reason
you're in Los Angeles.
Anticipating what hasn't yet
happened in a dream.
Sleeping in a circle
of fans with the dreamer.

Stella says, "Simon sez:
Do this!"
And she leans over the parapet
of the rope bridge,
1200 feet above
the El Dorado River,
her hair fluttering
in the dry currents
flowing up from the valley.
This is the place
where they play visitors
the chameleon's music
on long cold flutes.
Their ice-chip eyes glittering,
lizards scramble up the rockface
into crevices too narrow
to accommodate a human thumb.
Clutching her chauffeur's cap
and sucking on a plum pit,
you choose not to play
Simon Sez
with Stella just now.
Waves of clouds—

a curtain avocado-green
shot through with lemon—
are pushing over the horizon,
and despite the heat,
fish are jumping
in the river below:
something is going to happen,
you can feel it.
This morning a parcel
arrived from Hawaii:
six miniature pineapples—
not gold, but the real thing—
packed in white ferns
with a card that read:
WARMEST FELICITATIONS,
MADAMA BUTTERFLY.
The diva? The crazy woman?
The parcel was coffin-shaped,
with a coffin's proportions—
6 x 2 x 2—
and the pineapples,
with their frozen hearts,
were waxy to the touch,
like a corpse.
You remember on that same
trip to France discovering
the odd painting of Charles II
being presented with the first
pineapple grown on English soil,
the royal gardener, Mr. Rose,
genuflecting, proffering the fruit
on a burgundy cushion.
That pineapple was equally
cold and small,
and the debauched king,
gazing balefully at the artist,
had dressed in black

for the occasion.
In downtown L.A. the street gangs
have expanded their arsenals
to include machine guns,
armor-piercing bullets
and incendiary hand-grenades—
the latter commonly referred
to as *pineapples*
(as in baseball it is a term
for zero, a string of 0's, *nada*).
Stella herself keeps two Uzi
scatterguns in the limo;
one under the front seat,
one in the trunk.
Pineapples shipped air-express,
heavily insured, she takes in stride.
Perhaps like the eclectic Jefferson,
who despite pressing duties managed
to introduce waffles, spaghetti,
and ice cream to the United States,
she has a knack for bizarre
combinations of food—
salmon roe on vanilla pancakes,
zucchini mousse pie with quinces,
cucumber-lichee cookies—
and preparing your picnic lunch
she sliced those pineapples
with a butcher knife
and sandwiched them between
pieces of banana bread
with watercress, corn relish and halvah.
You wash it all down at dusk
with *Swollen Donkeys*
(another of her concoctions—
tequila, mango juice and triple sec)
while cruising the freeways
watching the city catch fire

and listening to salsa,
thinking: this is the life.
That's what *you're* thinking.
But Stella's not talking much suddenly—
since you left the river gorge
she's been preoccupied,
running her tongue along
the back of her teeth
and squinting behind purple goggles,
driving even faster than usual,
not even keeping time
to the music with her thumbs
on the steering wheel—
as she usually does—
just glancing at her watch too often
and sipping from the thermos.
It's Friday finally
and she paced the balcony
all night smoking
and never came to bed.
The large moon, blood-orange,
was balanced atop the needle
tower at the oil refinery
near the mountains—
like one of those trick toys
street magicians assemble
through sleight of hand
for the children of the poor.
Stella, however, is no longer poor.
And despite her fluency
in all other matters,
her childhood is verboten
conversation-wise.
Mention that father who fished
her from the sea,
like Triton hoisting a Nereid,
the brine pouring from

his coppered beard;
or her mother who lost her mind
over the suicide of her ex-lover
the day Stella was born
(according to a remark
  Rocco let slip);
or her sister the Carmelite nun,
and you can expect Stella
to clam up, close her eyes,
slip on her white fedora
with the pink ribbon
and the curled-down brim,
and sail off alone
along some subterranean river.
She gave you the silent treatment
for several hours when you let on
that you'd thumbed through
the blue photo album.
"Some things are private,"
  she said finally, sprinkling
birdseed into the aviary.
"Maybe that's hard for you
  to remember now, when you think
you've lost everything."
Later she apologized,
but her words stung you.
Does Stella, your bodyguard
in name and spirit,
have your number down to
the last decimal point?
Do you really think
you've lost *everything*?
Some days before, dissecting
a Spanish melon (the yellow
pulp riddled with gold seeds,
like buckshot in a cloud),
scraping free the fluff

with a knife curved as a scimitar,
you glimpsed your eyes
reflected in the blade,
masked with a band of sunlight:
at that instant
you had a premonition,
not of loss exactly,
but of a subtle transformation . . .
Maybe not so subtle,
but certainly more sinister
than you ever thought possible;
for though generally
you haven't *done* much
of anything for weeks—
finalizing your divorce
and gambling and making love
to Stella and hiding out—
all that strange admixture
of furtive anticipation
and guilty pleasure
has had its effect:
you're not the same man
who stepped off that plane
a month ago,
into the vast glaring spaces
under a steel sky.
For you, this city too
has been transformed,
into a huge warren
of echoless rooms, pastel byways,
endless white boulevards,
and warm airways populated
by millions of odd birds,
not least among them
you and Stella, solitary nesters,
the nocturnal variety,
thrown together temporarily—

feeding habits erratic,
mating rituals casual,
life span brief . . .
And in Stella's case,
with a penchant for song.
Nightingales fill the pepper trees
around the empty lot
and launch their cantatas
punctually at 1 A.M.
Last night while she paced
the balcony, you heard Stella
singing counterpoint to their harmonies,
her scratchy contralto trembling
into the higher registers
and then dissolving altogether.
Later, when you went out there
to bring her back to bed,
the steam from the streets
curling around your ankles
like a fine jungle mist,
she glowered at you
with a green glint—
a fiery splinter—
in her left eye.
You see it again
in the rearview mirror
as she negotiates the coast road
to San Pedro at 90 mph,
her unlined brow darkened
violet beneath the chauffeur's cap.
You stretch out your legs
and nestle your head deep
into the plush leather cushion
with its cold smell—
for even with all
that has passed between you,
Stella insists you sit

in the back while she drives.
You are still a client, after all.
And this night you feel
like a client.
Someone in a limo walled in
by dark glass en route
to a wedding, or a funeral;
somebody else's wedding,
your own funeral.
How much have you changed?
For one thing, you're packing
a rod too now, fully loaded,
Stella's spare .38—
the pearl handle inlaid
with a silver sea horse—
which she insists you carry tonight.
When you inquire about
this added precaution,
she shakes her head slowly.
"Trust me," she murmurs.
Tracing the outline of this weapon
in your jacket pocket,
you remember an item you saw
on the clock-TV at dawn
while with one eye
watching Stella towel herself
through the bathroom door
(in slow-motion tamping
shoulders, breasts, thighs,
her eyes closed,
her drenched hair clinging
to her back).
It seems that last night
a new galaxy, 300 times
the size of the Milky Way,
was discovered by astronomers
in New Mexico.

From the red desert
they pinpointed a stellar
nova shooting jagged red bolts—
"like a million thermonuclear bombs"—
into the icy blackness.
That light started traveling
earthward three centuries
after Christ's crucifixion,
during the reigns of Diocletian
and the first Tsin emperor,
and only this afternoon
entered your pupil
for the second time
in twelve hours from a grimy
television screen in Benny Benitez's
Shell station in Corona
when Stella stopped for gas.
Now as you pass the refinery
where the moon rested
on the needle, scarlet flares
shoot into the sky from a triple
row of high silver pipes—
as if a mad organist somewhere
underground is playing a fugue
on a keyboard of burning coals,
his fingers (like Hindu holy men)
dancing through arpeggios unscathed,
sending forth bursts of flame
rather than notes.
Skirting an obscure neighborhood
where (despite clear skies)
all the pedestrians are dressed
for a torrential downpour,
you zip across a suspension
bridge overlooking the site
of the shantytown
near the phantom library;

except that now the Belinsky Circus—
Rocco's employer and fellow-litigant,
Stella informs you—
is sprawled over the dusty acreage.
The lean-tos and army-surplus
tents have been replaced
by big-top tents, electric rides,
sideshow booths, and a caravan
of diesel trailers.
"We have time to kill,"
Stella says glumly,
"San Pedro's only an hour from here.
How about a little detour?"
You follow a dizzying succession
of overpasses, underpasses and spirals—
every variety of cement curly-Q—
and within minutes emerge
at ground-level staring up
into the nets of colored lights
that canopy the parking lot.
Seeing the circus' name
lit up in metallic blue
jars your memory,
and just as the recurrent dream
that has been bringing you out
of bed every night in a cold
sweat comes into focus,
you remember where you last
heard the name Belinsky.
"That teenager," you mutter,
"the widow of the junkyard tycoon—"
and Stella cuts you off
with a grimace.
"The one who threw the party,"
she nods wearily,
"and had her pineapples ripped off.
This circus was one of her husband's

investments—his hobby.
Nominally she's Rocco's boss,
though she takes no interest
in the operation.
They settled out of court
yesterday, by the way;
he won, and he's back at work,
but as soon as his contract's up
he'll be blacklisted for life.
I have a feeling the widow
may be here tonight."
Maybe so.
Otherwise, she can be found
in your nightmare,
playing a supporting role
in a disguise so transparent
it's foolproof.

It goes like this.
You're in a big house,
imitation Tudor inside a maze
of hedges, with a stone wall
and electrified gates
and acres of birches
filled with blackbirds.
In the oval at the head
of the driveway
there is an ornate fountain,
and at its center,
backdropped with golden spray,
a statue of a young girl—
maybe fifteen—naked,
riding astride two dolphins;
thin streams of milky water
jet from her nipples

and arc across the deep pool—
over marble satyrs
and mermaids on lily pads
and gilded reeds studded with jade,
and turtles, snails, and frogs
cast in bronze—
into the gaping mouth of a Centaur.
You're waiting for someone
in the library.
Every book is bound
in black morocco,
and after pulling one randomly
(*Flora of the Baja*)
and studying a glossy
illustration of a red cactus
dotted with human eyes,
you fix your gaze
on a portrait of the owners
of this house;
rendered in garish oils,
an old man and a teenage girl
who closely resemble the Centaur
and Nymph in the fountain.
Examining this painting
in a mirror across the room—
the tinted, quincuncial windows
distorting the sunlight
and checkering the walls emerald—
you lose track of the time.
Voices reverberate in distant chambers,
and you hear a violin & viola
duet through the ceiling,
and the crystal in the credenza
vibrates to tremors from below
that you cannot feel
through the delicate layers
of nerves in your feet.

Below shelves of bright artifacts,
and ebony death-masks,
six gold pineapples are displayed
in a glass cabinet
under tiny spotlights.
Though it is summer,
and the windows are beaded
with humidity, a huge fire
rages in the walk-in fireplace.
Suddenly you hear a rushing wind
in the hallway and the door
flies open and a young woman
in diaphanous harem robes
and a black veil,
with eyes heavily mascara'd
and a fiery wig and a necklace
strung with snake bones,
slithers in like Salome.
She's carrying something under
a fringed cloth on a silk pillow.
Her eyes are smiling wickedly
and her breasts press hard
against the sheer bodice.
She prances over to you
(frozen beside the fireplace,
the logs crackling waist-high)
and, hissing through her teeth,
with a flourish lifts
the cloth and you reel,
as if you're spinning down
from a tremendous height
into an ocean of lava:
for there on the pillow,
eyes gazing upward
like a blind man's,
the oiled hair perfectly combed,
the parted lips crusted with blood,

it is not the Centaur's head
she is serving up to you,
but your own!
Before you can recoil,
she flings it into the fire
and with a wild shriek
leaps for your throat.
As her long fingers choke you,
thousands of birds crash
through the windows
and you wake, the sweat
pouring into your eyes.
And last night
you dreamt it twice.

The circus is jammed.
In gaudy pools of purple
and magenta light, you pause
to watch the high-wire act—
four men on two unicycles
performing 200 feet up
without a net—
and the girl costumed as Annie Oakley
riding on a tiger's back,
the clowns with popguns
in metal drums tumbling
through a maze of booby traps,
the fire-eater in a rajah's robes,
the "Underwater Snake Lady,"
and of course Rocco
the Human Cannonball,
wearing a red luminescent
jumpsuit and red helmet.
He waves to you and Stella
as he approaches his cannon,

ascends a stepladder
and, on his stomach, disappears
feet-first down the 90-cm barrel
tilted at a 45-degree angle.
His assistant, a kewpie doll
in silver sequins and stiletto
heels, spins 360 degrees,
mugging for the crowd,
and sets a long torch
to a bogus fuse.
You can hear it sizzle down,
the crowd hushed
and the muffled drumroll
climaxing in a crash of cymbals
and a cloud of smoke
as Rocco explodes from the cannon
and sails over the center ring,
a hefty projectile climbing
a fast parabola
through the upper reaches
of the huge tent,
and then amid gasps and screams
plummeting to a small net,
bouncing—once, twice—
and flipping to his feet
under a wave of applause.
You're riveted, but Stella
is already walking away—
her mind is elsewhere,
she's seen his act many times—
and you follow her through
the overheated throngs
outside the animal cages—
restless panthers, sullen gorillas,
zebras saddled for a sextette
of equestrian ballerinas—
straight to the fortune-tellers'

are at odds with one another.
For once she's frightened.
And Rocco is pretending
(unconvincingly) that this
is not so, and neither
is pausing long enough
to take in the full import
of the other's messages.
So along a quavering blue current
from the limo to the motorcycle,
their muted telepathic voices
travel faster than light:
faster than the pinpoint starlight
that shoots back to the past
like a glowing thread
sixteen centuries long;
and the dull light around
the abandoned beach houses
that seeps into the future;
and the stiff revolving lighthouse
beam that vainly attempts
to illuminate the present.
No town on this coast,
no place on this spinning globe,
can be more opaque than San Pedro.
If landscapes are canvases,
the medium here is not
paint, but tar.
Sky, sea, cliffs—
each blacker than the last.
So the bats that halo the pines
and the mosquitoes clotting
the high-beam lights
are mere scraps and particles
of the night air come to life.
The wind scuds tumbleweed
across the road

and ripples the dune grass
at the foot of the cliffs—
like another, quieter sea.
On the true sea a buoy clangs.
The high tide is receding.
The deep water piped to shore
through hidden channels
deposited nautilus shells
lined with onyx;
and silver pebbles chipped
from the enormous mirror
that covers the seafloor;
and the limpid remains
of blind deep-sea creatures
that glide over that mirror
searching for their own images.
Speeding to the edge of the cliff,
Stella parks the limo between
two limestone boulders
and rapidly unclips and examines
the cartridge from her .38,
then snaps it back in place,
her eyes smoky, like platinum,
as she stares out to sea.
Somewhere along that last stretch
Rocco and the motorcycle
disappeared without a trace,
so it's only the two
of you clambering down
the rough winding path
to the ribbon of beach.
There, on the very edge
of the continent,
you ask yourself what Jefferson
would have thought had soothsayers
(like the Romanians)
informed him that western expansion—

Manifest Destiny—
in the United States would reach
beyond California, clear across
the vast marine prairies to Hawaii.
And catching the heel
of your snakeskin cowboy boot
between two shards of limestone
(like Proust, stepping on
the uneven cobblestone),
you reel as the horizon parts
like a curtain and delirious
vistas open out before you;
you envision a floral tapestry
extending the length of the Pacific,
centered at 21°N, 157°W
in the floating Babylonian Gardens
in Honolulu, a stone's throw
from the oldest cemetery on Oahu,
named after St. Kieran
(who rose from the dead
for twenty-four hours
to perform miracles)
and ringed on three sides
by pineapple groves.
You see pipers playing reeds
cut from a river warmer
than blood, and legions
of the dead shrouded in mist
and wingéd like butterflies
sleeping in the acacia trees.
All the graves are empty,
and when nimbus clouds roil in
from the sea, and thunder batters
every drum in the sky,
the ensuing deluge is not
of rain, but flowers,
filling the graves to overflowing.

You lift your heel from the shards
and the flowers evaporate . . .
Only seconds have elapsed.
In the darkness down the dangerous
spiral, your eyes are glued to
Stella's taut, well-shaped ass—
worthy of the goddess Shiva,
or Pallas Athena, sprung from
her father's head wearing
an iron bra and armored G-string,
or that Aztec corn goddess
who brandished a sword
in each hand, her irises
smoldering with mauve embers.
Finally Stella breaks her silence,
calling over her shoulder,
"Simon sez—do this!"
And turning a pair of perfect
cartwheels, she somersaults off
the last bend in the path
and lands nimbly on the sand.
You applaud softly,
but she never glances back—
she's striding straight for the water.
It's 9:45: you're early.
And there's no one on the beach.

"**10:10,**" Stella mutters,
the numerals on her watch gleaming,
and as you crouch there together
in the grass surveying
the windswept beach,
you think about the fact
that except for the policeman
and the blind man playing darts,

you didn't see another
living soul in San Pedro—
and not a car in either direction
on the road
from the main highway.
Is this one of those ghost towns
(complete with tumbleweed & bats)
Stella told you about that night
you met the Romanians
at the widow Belinsky's party?
"You got it," Stella whispers,
leaping into your thoughts.
"We may not be in New Mexico,
but this is the next best thing."
Astonished for the last time
by her telepathic powers,
you jump up, but she grabs
your arm and pulls you back.
"Shhh, they're here,"
she snaps, her face grim.
At first you can't see a thing—
then the clouds break around
that lucent, petaled moon,
and following Stella's cat-like
gaze through the sharply
rustling grass, you freeze:
close enough to touch,
a man and a woman, rigid as statues,
are inked against the shadows
wearing hooded capes;
and in the distance another couple—
the man leaning on a shovel
and the woman wearing a Stetson
and twirling an umbrella—
are standing arm-in-arm;
and at the water's edge
a third man, in a turban,

is tossing a piece of driftwood
which a black dog obediently
fetches from the surf.
From where you sit,
the two couples
and the man with the dog
form an equilateral triangle
at the center of which
a shiny anchor lies half-buried
in the sand, connected to
the sea by a long chain.
The hooded couple are first
to move: dropping their capes,
they cross to the anchor,
passing through a shaft of moonlight;
they're small and dark,
the woman busty and erect,
the man barrel-chested
with a bushy moustache.
"The Romanians," you whisper,
turning around, only to discover
that Stella has disappeared;
at the same instant,
your heart thumping somewhere
outside your body,
you notice that the woman
with the umbrella,
who could be either
the widow Belinsky
or the crazy woman—
or both—is also gone.
The man with the shovel
is approaching the anchor,
limping, but you can't
yet make out his face.
And where is Stella?
Gripping her spare .38

in your pocket,
you wipe the sweat
from your brow.
The Romanians, both
in men's clothing, look
as if they have just stepped
from a Philadelphia street
in 1800—tails, ruffled
shirts, and three-point hats—
and to your surpise
the diva is launching into
Elvira's lament from *Don Giovanni*,
her voice trailing in the wind,
her despairing face turned
to the fast sky.
The man with the shovel
stops in his tracks
and you recognize Z. Zimmer
in a policeman's uniform.
A policeman playing a policeman.
The waves are thrashing in
harder now, and you realize
the man in the turban
and the dog have also disappeared.
As the diva hits the higher
registers, standing back-to-back
with her husband by the anchor,
you wonder if he's going to respond
in a resonant baritone,
to assume the role of Don Giovanni,
the man of folly (your role!),
but, no, when she's finished
he coolly takes a flintlock
pistol from his belt,
cocks it, and raises his arm
toward the stars.
The diva does the same,

and they begin walking stiffly
in opposite directions,
stepping off exactly ten paces,
then wheeling around;
she fires into the air,
but her husband shoots directly
at her chest—a blank—
and it hits you
that they are reenacting
the fateful duel at
Weehawken Heights, New Jersey,
between Hamilton (Jefferson's archenemy)
and Burr (his flawed surrogate),
a duel that, mentally speaking,
Hamilton and Jefferson rehearsed
many times in the feverish
swampy air of the Potomac
during the early days
of the Republic.
But why this pantomime?
To summon forth *his* ghost?
And is this the inspiriting
element in the turbulent winds,
the inverted cone trembling
on its axis like a cyclone
that whirls in from sea
and spins up onto the cliffs?
It opens like a chrysalis
and reveals a luminous figure
who stands with arms upraised
and face on fire, gazing eastward—
maybe clear over the earth's
curvature to the other side
of the continent, the other sea,
where the waves break high and cold.
And then, just as quickly,
the winds cocoon him again

and fly back over
the horizon like a top.
The Romanians are on their knees,
shielding their eyes and singing
a duet, and you're prostrate,
your insides quaking.
When that cyclone passed
over you again,
it was studded with human eyes.
Like a peacock's tail.
Like the cactus in your dream.
But was the apparition on the cliff
really Jefferson's ghost?
And how did a man with his brains
ever become President, anyway?
(Chosen over Burr, in fact,
after Hamilton's intervention,
by the House of Representatives—
"the lesser of two evils";
this trio rivaling any
in Tacitus's Rome . . .)
Z. Zimmer, meanwhile,
blows his police whistle,
pitches his shovel into
the sand beside the anchor,
and starts digging.
You think perhaps the time
has come for you to circle
around to the cliffs yourself
and wait for Stella by the limo,
but just as you start out
you glimpse the woman
with the umbrella poised
on one knee at the edge
of the grass, waiting for you,
something in her right hand flashing . . .
Ducking your head down,

you plunge in the other direction,
toward the sea,
where the lighthouse beam
dances over the leaden waves.
Far up the beach, you hear
the dog barking again.
You run hard and twice stumble,
catching yourself inches
from a fall, your boot soles
slick on the slippery dunes,
and only when you've veered
onto the packed wet sand,
splashing through the foam,
do you pick up speed.
Sunbathing on Stella's roof,
you asked yourself if you were
Chuang Tzu's butterfly dreaming
of yourself as a man;
maybe now, sprinting through
the moist, poisonous darkness,
you'll learn that one day
you're going to start dreaming
of yourself as a butterfly
only to finish as a man
and there won't be any line
of demarcation—you'll cross
from one dream to the other
without conscious thought:
like death.
But not tonight. Not now.
For suddenly, out of the spray,
a woman steps into your path
brandishing a revolver.
A necklace of snake bones
jangles around her throat,
and through the mist
that veils her face

those wicked eyes
from your dream are glowing
with a cold fire.
Running toward you from the beach,
Z. Zimmer is shouting,
"It's her, it's her!"
"It's me, all right," she says
in a razor voice,
gliding towards you.
"I'll give you five seconds
to get out your gun."
But you're transfixed,
and as a gust of wind dispels
the mist, you find yourself
face to face with Stella,
her hair blowing out wild
and the surf crackling
at your feet like fire.
Fingering the snake necklace
with her free hand,
she levels the revolver
at your heart and smiles.
"I was Salome in your dream.
I'm the one who's been after you.
Let's do something crazy.
Simon sez—do this!"
And as her finger squeezes
the trigger, a shot
rings out, a bolt of ice
impales your gut,
and you watch Stella stagger
back into the waves,
her face blank,
her black pupils expanding,
flooding her face
with deathly shadows—
like a pair of islands

under a tidal wave.
Blood trickling from her mouth,
she dives into the closing
arc of the next breaker
and another shot explodes
at close range
and all the lights go out—
starlight, moonlight, lighthouse.

After an eternity—
maybe five minutes later—
Rocco, in the turban,
is cradling your head,
a smear of blood on his cheek.
"We have to get out of here,"
he says, lifting you
to your feet and leading
you across the sand.
Z. Zimmer, his .45 smoking
at his side, his white
moustache twitching, is walking
ahead of you sullenly.
Now he's wearing the Stetson.
His black dog is howling
at the waves,
but there's no sign
of Stella anywhere.
Beside the anchor, the Romanians
are drawing a chest out
of a hole which is large
enough to be a grave.
It is a grave, 6 x 2 x 2.
But Rocco, gripping your arm,
won't let you get close
enough to peer in.
"I'm convinced," Z. Zimmer drawls,

"that those two are legit.
That was no normal cyclone,
and there's not a bunko dick
in the country who'd say otherwise.
I still ought to take 'em in,
as a formality,
but who's to say
I ever saw 'em tonight—
or that anything happened here?
Who's to say any of us
were here at all?"
The widow Belinsky, sans umbrella,
is taking fistfuls of freesia
from inside her cloak
and tossing them into the grave.
with a bowie knife Z. Zimmer
pries open the chest,
removes six gold pineapples
(one for each of you on the beach?)
packed snugly in cotton,
presents them to the widow,
and starts refilling the grave
with help from his dog.
The Romanians don their capes,
and taking advantage of Zimmer's
beneficent blind eye,
slip away into the night.
The widow, pulling her cloak tight,
lights a clove cigarette.
Watching her waft smoke rings
up around the moon,
your legs already rubbery,
you grow dizzier and dizzier,
and the next thing you know
Rocco is hustling you up
the cliff along the winding path.
When you reach the limo,

he takes the .38 from your pocket
and hurls it across the road.
You glance out over the beach
and there's not a sign of life—
just that half-buried anchor
beside the freshly turned sand—
marking what? Whose grave?
Overhead, the bats are swarming
back to their caves
and the lighthouse beam
has been turned landward,
into the mountains.
Rocco, stone-faced, unlocks
the trunk and removes a steel suitcase.
For the first time, you realize
his turban is part of an elaborate
fortune-teller's costume—
pantaloons, a gold silk vest
embroidered with the signs of
the zodiac, and red dervish slippers.
Your first day in L.A.
it was Stella who told you
your fortune; the Romanians
never had the chance;
and now maybe it's up to
Rocco to seal your fate.
You're woozy and scared
as he releases the catch
and opens the suitcase—
but, no, it contains,
not another lethal weapon,
but a black chauffeur's uniform,
complete with hat and shiny boots,
and Rocco changes before
your eyes in a flash.
Now does he plug you,
stuff your body into the trunk

and ditch it in some ravine?
Wrong again. You seem to have
missed the point entirely:
you're still the client here
(with as much control over
events as you ever had—
which is to say, very little),
and you're simply being taken
for one last ride.
After depositing you
in the rear seat,
Rocco flicks on the headlights
and you're jolted at the sight
of a man's profile scorched
onto one of the boulders.
A profile you've seen
thousands of times—
in phone booths, video arcades,
and candy stores when you were a kid—
cameo'd on U.S. nickels.
Jefferson's profile.
And then the limestone goes blank
as Rocco executes a lightning
U-turn, kicking up gravel,
and you speed back
through San Pedro
(where the café and police station
are also in darkness now),
north on Route 1, straight
to L.A. International Airport.
For many miles Rocco
does not look away
from the purple ribbon
bisected with the Morse code
of the lane-markers,
his eyes concealed
(as Stella's so often were)

by the brim of his cap.
Your skull is pounding
and you discover a walnut-sized
lump behind your ear
where someone must have slugged you,
but gradually your dizziness
spirals down to your feet
and flies from your body,
and the frigid jets
streaming from the air-conditioning
vents clear your head.
While passing a caravan
of trailer trucks heading south,
you sit up and take a swig
from the silver flask
Stella gave you, the truck
headlamps shooting through
the limo's tinted windows
and exploding around you and Rocco
like phosphorescent flares,
and out of your hundreds
of questions, you ask him one—
the biggest one after all
you've seen and heard this night:
"Why did she do it?"
It takes him a long time to answer.
"All she told me," he replies gruffly,
"was that she knew you
intimately in another life,
and she had a score to settle.
You know she believed in
that stuff, just like Zimmer
and the others . . . .
Why did she wait so long?
Because in these things
there's always a right time and place:
the place was San Pedro,

the time was tonight."
He shakes his head.
"Also, you were right:
there *was* a contract out for you
after you won big in Vegas.
You crossed the wrong people.
That guy in Tahoe who sent you
to Stella—he was mob.
But that wasn't why she did it.
Fact is, despite everything,
she told me she was falling
in love with you."
It takes you a while—
and several more pulls of tequila—
to digest all this.
You lean forward and grip
the top of the front seat.
"And you, Rocco, do you believe
in that stuff, too, like Zimmer—
and who the hell is he, anyway?"
For nearly five miles Rocco
doesn't respond, and by now
you're on the outskirts of the city,
the factory lights twinkling
through thick bands
of green and gold air—
as if you're driving across
Saturn's rings, racing
into the heart of the planet,
which someone once told you
is a sea of gasoline,
with tides, currents, and who
knows what sorts of life forms
traversing its depths—
when suddenly Rocco answers you.
"Forget Zimmer," he says softly.
"And I already told you:

It's like people who believe
in God, or people in love:
they don't even have
to think about it.
But people with nothing always
have plenty to think about.
That's what I believe."

These are not his last words
of wisdom for you.
At the gate, he hands you
your ticket and boarding pass
and looks at you squarely
with his bullet eyes,
pushing back his cap
and showing his teeth,
the canines capped in gold:
"Better not come back
here for a while."
Then he turns on his heel
and disappears into the crowd,
and within twenty minutes
you're airborne, rumpled,
with no baggage, rain
streaking the oval window
as you pass over the coastline,
flying due west,
to the true edge of the USA,
2500 miles at sea,
halfway to the East
yet away from the rising sun
which six hours later
is shooting crimson streaks
into the sky and bombarding
the Alaska-Hawaii Time Zone

with deadly gamma rays
that penetrate the ozone layer
and the jet's steel skin
and bathe your cranium
with a pink fluorescence
as the pilot announces your descent
into Honolulu Airport,
the runway sparkling with dew.
Outside the terminal
a white sedan is waiting
for you by the taxi-queue.
A woman is behind the wheel.
You slide into the rear seat
without seeing her face
and she accelerates
quickly down the ramp.
Strands of seaweed are braided
into her long hair.
At your feet, in a puddle
of saltwater, a piece of kelp
is looped into a figure-eight.
Your tongue lies numb
and your limbs are like iron.
And at the instant
you glimpse her eyes
in the rearview mirror,
the powerful scent of freesia
fills your nostrils,
and the familiar voices
of strangers, and of the dead
who have become strangers
wash over you in waves,
and as the landscape
drains of color
and the colors flood your heart,
you close your eyes
and you can see.

II..................

KRAZY KAT

Playing the bongos in Rome,
dancing the rumba in Reykjavík—
he's seen it all, from Oslo to Oman.

From the Tarot deck, he always draws
the Knave of Batons:
trustworthy and doomed to misadventure.

He's so wired, with so many outlets
into the expanding universe,
that he can't connect with anyone anymore.

On a supersonic jet over the Sahara,
Mahler rumbling on his earphones,
he sets up his magnetic chess set.

From memory, he plays out Alekhine's
famous victory over Capablanca at Leiden
in 1938, using the French Defense.

He can still smell dates frying in oil
at the bazaar in Rabat, and he can taste
the wind flooding the *medina*, dark as honey.

But he hasn't talked to a soul in days.
His pockets are filled with cigarettes,
candy bars, and maps of the seafloor.

Once he owned a globe of Mars—
its mountain ranges cleverly embossed—
charted as minutely as the USA.

So when the first astronaut zips across
the red planet in his dune buggy
he'll know exactly where he's going.

Everything will have a name.
Like this lissome stewardess behind her veil.
And the desert below. And the pink stars.

At the airport in Tunis, he drinks
mint juleps in the empty VIP lounge;
twice in two weeks the place has been bombed.

Cops in mufti eye him closely
in his black Stetson, puffing a corona,
a copy of the Koran in his hip pocket.

He's just skimmed the first chapter—
"Thick Blood, or Clots of Blood"—
trying to find the epigrams the terrorists use.

4000 years ago, Pharoah's cats gazed on
the blue world and cried for grief all night.
Krazy Kat can relate to this.

In the name of Allah, the compassionate, the merciful:
in the end how do we know one desert from another,
and how do we remember our own names?

He's sure that on Mars those red canals
flow south to north, like the Nile,
thick as lava and cold as human blood.

COLLECTING STAMPS IN
PORT-AU-PRINCE

Here's another dictator with a bright blue
parrot on his shoulder, white top hat, and sash
blazing forth the colors of the Republic.
A departure from those tedious series of sailboats,
sunsets, and gay fishermen that enchanted the previous rulers.
This fellow's grandfather, one-time "emperor," with a retinue
of forty pugilists in baseball caps and sunglasses,
was a good friend to the orphans of the capital
and every Christmas presented them with shoes and socks,
then picked out the prettiest girl, took her
to the honeymoon suite of the King James Hotel,
and kept her in thrall for a year.
He had forty-seven such brides during his reign
which ended when #4, an aging consumptive,
emerged from obscurity and shot him in the confession box.
His son and grandson were never so careless.
They didn't advertise their peccadilloes,
rarely attended church, and never confessed to anything.
When they issued commemorative sheets to trumpet
the virtues of their regimes, they kept them simple:
banana trees in pink sunlight, canoeists in dusky lagoons,
jai alai players, and flattering self-portraits.
The son was himself an amateur collector;
he hosted the first Transcaribbean Philatelic Convention,
and his albums are displayed at the National Museum
alongside his sabers, crowns, and the 689 medals
for valor he awarded himself.
Every year on her birthday he decreed a stamp
to honor his wife, a former cabaret hostess,
costumed variously as Pallas Athena and Marie Antoinette.
The grandson (the one with the parrot) in the end
went kinky, like his grandfather, manning a destroyer

with an all-girl crew, bathing beauties in seamen's uniforms,
and chasing them around the deck by moonlight;
he drowned on one such outing, wrestling two "mermaids,"
and, miraculously, when his body washed up the next morning,
it was festooned with orchids and surrounded by dolphins,
his white admiral's uniform still crisp and dry.
Even today his sinister countenance,
under that top hat, sees every letter on the island,
from the rustiest post box on the remotest country lane,
to its ultimate destination, worldwide,
though most of the stamps are so gorgeously intricate
that the addressee forgets to open his mail,
oddly reminding us of those old movies
in which the dizzy blonde or the mischievous upstart
sticks a rare stamp on an envelope
and hands it to the mailman so the comedy might begin,
the complex machinations of recovering the stamp
before it is postmarked, while the letter within
(which might contain crucial information—
of lost love or riches or intrigue)
is utterly forgotten.

GREEN ANIMALS

You can glimpse them at twilight
in the vague terrain surrounding
the ancient stadium after it rains;
or on the cupola's copper dome,
weathered the acid-green of the sea
at dawn, before the storm comes.

When they stare back at you,
you see the eyes of your ancestors glittering,
their familiar forms unlike those
you imagined for the dead
in their sky-locked rooms;
you see yourself in those blurred settings,
before a forest backdropped with mountains.
Beyond all that, and beyond still
more mountains and an emerald sea,
lies a greener landscape
from which the animals have fled
in a vast cloud, like ghosts.
Call it death, something permanent,
as you listen to the rain approaching
fast across the hollow rooftops.

VOYEUR

Like the ghost of a ghost, the woman
in the apartment across the street
floats through her living room
clutching a whiskey bottle and a candle.
She's wearing a silk robe, stained
at the cuffs, glass slippers,
and a gray homburg with a pink ribbon.
It's 4 A.M. and she's got calypso music
throbbing on the stereo, bringing on
the lights in the neighboring apartments.
They've called the cops on her before;
from her terrace, in a driving rain,
she pelted the squad car with eggs.
I've only seen her once in the neighborhood,
four years ago, at the bakery, a demure
young businesswoman in a stylish trenchcoat,
the *Times* bulging out of her tennis bag.
Back then, she didn't live alone.
First there was an older man (he resembled
Toscanini) who smoked cheroots and wore a fez,
and after dinner played the bassoon;
and then a Korean girl who twice daily
did her t'ai chi exercises
on the terrace in purple tights.
Often the two women dressed up like Kabuki
dancers—white face, severe makeup,
robes and fans—and performed a ritual
striptease before a blue screen,
always ending up in a tangled embrace
down the hallway, just out of sight.
For a while she threw raucous parties,
then gradually started drinking alone.

She usually passes out in front of
the television, but tonight must be
one of those negative anniversaries
that clutter a drunk's calendar.
For hours she's prowled her apartment
with the candle, searching—behind books
and furniture, drawers and closets—
for *something*, the long-lost piece
of the enormous jigsaw puzzle that,
once completed, will displace her insomnia
with a panoramic vision of her life
as it will never be.
At dawn she staggers out onto
the terrace, the candle guttering
and the cold light blanching her face.
With a flick of the wrist, she tosses
the homburg and it sails down
onto the hood of a cab;
the driver slams on his brakes
and she applauds—then suddenly
looks over at me and waves:
the first time ever
she has acknowledged my presence.
As if for all these years
she has known there was someone
in the window mirroring her own—
as if by observing her performance
I have been giving one myself.
Before I can step back, she is gone,
her robe draped over the railing,
and on the street a bag-woman
in a soiled raincoat snatches up
the homburg with a flourish
and glances at the windows above,
the wind knocking her off-balance
as she rounds the corner.

ELEGY FOR
MY GRANDMOTHER

Now you're in the place where the shadows fly,
light-years away from this palm forest—
the room I've taken overlooking the Caribbean,
macaws squawking at the stars
and coconuts thudding to earth.

At your old house the garden lies barren;
lightning split the cherry trees,
black vines choked the azaleas.
You were famous for your green thumb.
Neighbors brought you their ailing plants,
and after a week on your terrace
the puniest amaryllis turned prodigy.
Your bags were always packed:
you loved to travel first-class, to sail
south at the earliest sign of winter.
I have a photograph of you in prewar Havana
wearing a white coat and feathered hat
after a day at the races,
gazing to sea (these same flashing waters)
from the casino balcony.
I remember you were cursed
with eyesight so sharp it daggered
migraines through your temples.
Once, driving in the country, you glanced
at a distant forest—
a blue band across the hills—
and counted the crows on a single bough.

You were first onto the dance floor
when the music started—and last to sit.
Before I could read, you taught me

poems and riddles, and those intricate
parables with the quirky endings—
your own variations on some theme.
You knew the real theme is always death,
and when I was ten you explained it to me:
one is on an enormous ship
(lush gardens lining the decks)
gliding over a white sea that never ends.
There is no horizon, no sun or moon:
the air is purest light.
The portholes are mirrors,
full of glittering expanses.
Somewhere on board an orchestra
is playing beautiful music,
but no one can find the musicians. . . .

Now that you're a passenger on that ship,
sailing and sailing into the light,
are they playing for you
on a dance floor strewn with flowers,
and is the music really so beautiful?
Nana, this was your way of telling me
you would never come back.

CIRCE REVISITED

She arranges starflowers in a black vase
and sets the table for three.
The silverware is embossed with falcons.
Icy violins are playing on the phonograph.

I'm leafing through a guidebook to
the planetarium in Milan, where I first met her;
it says there may be diamonds
the size of boulders in Saturn's rings.

Her cats stare at me from the couch
as she removes her teardrop earrings,
slips them into a glass of champagne
and raises it high, so the diamonds

catch the flames from the fireplace.
"The last time I saw you," she smiles,
"I dreamt we were in a forest,
embracing at the bottom of a cold lake."

Unzipping her dress, she lets her hair
down and slips off her shoes.
Her feet glow like marble.
Snow is blowing against the window.

In the shadows I feel as if we're underwater
and I'm trying to swim away from her.
She tinkles the earrings in her glass
and beckons me closer.
"Hurry, before he gets home . . .
and don't ever try to leave me again."

MIRANDA IN RENO

In a silent room surrounded by sand I sleep.
Sometimes the phantoms of the dead
on the far shore wrestle for hours
with the great questions he and I—
and everyone we had ever forgotten—
abandoned when we fell out of love,
when the long nights appropriated us.

Or maybe they aren't phantoms.
It's winter on that island, the frozen
snow is bricked high for miles,
like a seawall to discourage visitors:
in spring it will thaw, the beach will flood,
and the actors masquerading as ghosts will drown.

To marry means to halve one's rights & double one's duty.
Or as a friend observed at his ex-wife's wedding:
divorces open out, marriages close in.
Really both are imaginary lines over which
two briefly parallel lines intersect,
creating a rectangle—a cell.
Everyone I know is drowning trying to escape some island.

Other times, the dead on their milky shore
rock in unison in marble chairs
and agree that the great questions
were so many distractions they erected
like a long white wall to keep themselves
from falling too deeply in love.

Last night in the dry stillness I dreamt
of that island again: the snow fell fast

and under the ice the drowned men recited
their lines, scripted subtly by my former husband.
It's true, you see, they aren't phantoms.
But who can say how I came to this desert,
all my lights burning at noon, and the phone—
off the hook for days—ringing again.

THE HOTTEST NIGHT OF THE YEAR

The steam never lifts on lower Broadway.
Shadows clash behind dirty glass
and the asphalt smolders after a week of rain.
Bums in semicircle (lounging, as in Plato's banquet)
pass their wine under a line of windows
marked SHAFTWAY at every floor.
Is this posted to prevent our falling in?
And who put windows there in the first place?
Like the leggy girl at the phone booth
twirling her umbrella, faking tears,
or the sailors sleeping in a pink limousine,
the shaftway teases up more questions
than can be answered in the course
of a single block,
so it is a relief to turn the corner
and confront fresh distractions
and possible historic landmarks
(did Poe stride past this blackened foundry—
"1840" chiseled in the eaves—
or smoke under this seashell
portal on another sweltering night?),
and we find our preoccupations of the day
deflected by a harmonica playing Handel down an alley;
and a woman's silhouette, fresh from the bath,
gliding behind curtains in a mansard roof;
and the truck labeled NOVELTIES overflowing
with inflatable ducks at a loading zone,
a couple in purple masks necking in the cab.
Is it the heat breeds such wonders?
One hundred and five and steady, these other
shadows like steaming pitch smeared around pedestrians,
air-conditioners wheezing and whining

in the static air, sapping the borough's electricity,
dimming millions of lamps.
Up at the stadium the athletes dance
in slow-motion, playing out their destinies,
and at the piers the fishermen
cast sizzling lines into the Hudson
while the jets scream in their holding patterns;
in this heat that speeds clocks and pulses
and prolongs criminal acts (like liquid
amber enveloping living things
in an instant of high temperature),
the ball game may dissolve into a free-for-all,
and the planes turn out to sea without fuel,
and the black bass swell into leviathans,
and we may never reach the café
we discovered one winter in a blizzard.
Adulterers then, married now,
we were attracted to the flashing sign
just above it—a beacon through the fierce snow—
flaming orange in the window of the walk-up church:
SINNERS WELCOME, NIGHT & DAY.
I wonder if we're still welcome—
lustful and passionate, our bellies roaring
with fire in this enormous furnace—
knowing that before the night is out
rain will hiss again on the terrible streets
and the gutters will run with lava,
and we'll thrash, you and I, like failing
swimmers, in our bed.

CHRISTMAS, 1956

They had him on a velveteen throne
in the toy department
beside a metal tree
sprayed with aerosol snow.
His cheeks were rouged
and there was a whiff
of onion on his breath
and a cookie crumb
stuck in his beard.
He looked like a man
who enjoyed boilermakers
and hero sandwiches
with all the trimmings.
He was nearsighted,
deep crow's-feet forking
from his washed-out eyes.
When he rang his bell,
we filed in one at a time,
sat on his lap,
and were photographed
by a skinny woman
dressed as an elf
who talked to herself.
I liked that he wore white
gloves with tiny buttons;
I liked his shiny belt
with the silver buckle.
But his boots were all wrong.
They weren't boots at all:
around his calves, above
scuffed, rubber-sole shoes,
he had fastened black

plastic cylinders with zippers.
He sported a watch, too,
with a radium dial
and a chromium Speidel band
that pinched his pudgy wrist.
A star-traveler such as he
(our first astronaut?),
able to navigate unerringly
in dead of night,
should have had no need
of such a primitive timepiece.
I told him what I wanted
him to bring me—
listed according to preference—
and he listened absently,
squinting into the light,
then gave me a candy cane
and sent me on my way.

Riding home, I figured that
even though every big store
in every city in America
employed one of these imposters,
though there must be thousands
of them with pillows
strapped around their waists
and fake beards glued
to their chins,
one and only one
(free to operate in secrecy
because of all his decoys)
had to be real.

THE STREET AT THE END OF THE RIVER

This is the street where the old men
get lost in the light.
Dry leaves whirl along the rooftops.
Marigolds puff out cold and yellow.
A dog sprawls on a grate
in a cloud of gnats, and the ghosts
of squirrels prowl the power lines.
From the river, the wind blows hard and low.
The doorways are thick with dust
and cobwebs curtain the windows.

This is the way things go here:
the sun creeps up behind the park
and plunges down over the river.
When somebody dies, the bells ring
in the church with the blue windows.
If no one has died, they still ring.
The light is so bright,
strung through the trees
like violin strings (trembling)
that it can make you dizzy.

If you lose your way,
give yourself up to the bells
and the buffeting wind—
though fear catches in your throat—
and with luck you may stumble
on an open door, a shining corridor,
even a room, tiled in gold,
with a bed to lie in
and music dark as the river
to guide you through your sleep.

THREE FORTUNES

I dine at a Thai restaurant
and maybe because I'm alone
they bring me three fortune cookies:
Avoid long entanglements
Temperance is your strong suit
Somewhere someone is speaking your name

Once, with you, I got a cookie
with no fortune inside—
remember?—and the waiter
assured me I'd have ten years
of fabulous luck or else would die
in my sleep that night.

He wasn't even close.
As strange as it is that you're
on the other side of the planet
gazing at a snowstorm from
a white room, and stranger still
that I'm exiled here like a blind man,

dark webs over my eyes and a cane
hooked to the back of my chair,
I saw something even stranger today
in the newspaper: did you know the Earth
is in a rare alignment with Mars,
Jupiter and Mercury which last occurred

when Antony slipped off with Cleopatra?
The hat-check girl at the hotel bar
told me it means no one can die

on the equator or at either pole
for the remainder of the week.
You see I still rely on casual sources,

plugged into their private networks,
for vital, even cosmic, information.
They're refreshingly insulated
from the rigmarole of the highbrow types
with whom I frittered away so many years.

At night the wind swirls
through this city without a sound,
swaying the plane trees along the boulevards,
with their tinfoil leaves,
and flapping the policemen's capes
and gusting the fountains' spray
from plaza to plaza—

but no one can hear a thing.
It's not a good place to be alone.
Some places are—certain islands,
and the northern cities in winter—
though it depends on who you were with
before you were alone, and for how long.

Near my hotel I pass a phalanx
of horsemen in long coats,
their gray hats tilted low,
their voices carrying against the wind;
the horses' hooves stutter-step
silently on the cobbles.

I feel stronger, and in my dreams
walk for miles without the cane,
but I'm sure if I sailed to the equator
or were crazed enough to visit

the South or North Poles,
I would defy the hat-check girl's maxim.

As for these strips of tissue
paper unfurled from the interiors
of the cracked-open, conch-like cookies,
I suppose you've had a good laugh
over the first two;
it's the other one that troubles me

as I turn into an unlit street
where the empty doorways
gape black as the sea.
I shudder with the certainty
that someone somewhere is speaking my name
and I wonder if it's you

when suddenly I hear the wind rush
down the street, through the trees—
like a pursuer, pursuing me.

NOCTURNE FOR MIRANDA

Here are the blue tulips of sleep
about to open, just this once, for you.
No one else in the world can see them.

Doesn't that mean you're dreaming?
How else do you explain this single
white road that intersects all others,

and this river with hot & cold
tributaries connecting vast seas,
from the Indian Ocean to Baffin Bay.

Once again, you're at a crossroads,
a wellspring of promise and regret,
with not a stitch on your back

and no one to help you, when suddenly
you feel àn Arctic tingle
traveling the veins to your heart,

alerting you to dangers you never
foresaw in your waking life—
jaguars crouched to spring from

bronze foliage, and falcons
with talons like scythes
swooping out of purple clouds.

Someone inside your head inside
this dream is telling you
which direction to take for satori.

Light! And though no stars configure
this jet sky, and no moon floods
the fields with milky vapors,

there is still the possibility
you will find what you have been
searching for all these years,

something fierce and luminous
to cut through the snares
that have entangled your other dreams.

Just remember: the odds are against
your ever coming back to this place
at another moment so precipitous,

poised on the verge of destruction
(or more terrible enlightenment),
waiting for your heart to stop thumping

and for these tulips—lapis petals
flecked with gold—to open
just this once, before you wake.

CIRCE IN LOVE

Glancing away from the party of boisterous
men flushed and furious with wine,
a platter of ribs steaming before them,
she halves a pear and smiles grimly
at her companions. Across the dance floor,
a man is waiting for someone at a table for two.
He is middle-aged, with a red beard.
His clothes are foreign-cut and out of fashion.
Long voyages and bitter storms have lined his face.

On her island, with its lunar mountains,
it rains blue anemones at dawn.
The children eat black honey on black bread
and the old people are put to sea on hulks.
Amnesia is a national affliction.
No records are kept, no books printed.
In the schools they teach divination:
how to decipher the viscera
in which our destinies are scripted
and how to read the maps
the lost souls send back from hell.

But tonight, while rain furrows the windows
like acid, and half the men and women
in the world know they could die for love
and the other half know they will die
for nothing, she assures herself
this traveler is waiting for her.
Tossing her hair back to catch
the lights, she crosses the room,
weaving through the dancers slowly.
And the band, knowing her song, plays it slowly.

MAP

My great-grandfather was beached
in the tropics on Christmas Day, 1870,
redirecting the family destiny
(the geography shifted, the genes darkened);
still adrift at the end of a long life,
surrounded by mute children, he died
in a bamboo room, behind mosquito netting,
listening to his wife's chimes.
I visit his grandfather's hometown,
walk the narrow streets he walked,
loiter in the church where he was baptized,
married, and buried, where the icy statues
of the angels that survey the pews
were modeled on his twin daughters,
lost in a blizzard only to resurface
in Africa, as missionaries;
I have their picture tucked into my notebook,
blonde girls in severe coats, smiling.
Exploring the town, I feel as if I have
touched down from another planet;
it's hard to connect with these ghosts
whose blood fills my veins.
I cannot imagine what they would make of me,
unshaven, speaking a strange language,
dust-caked on a motorcycle.
The red sun burns slowly.
Snow shrouds the hills in lace.
Tucked into the river bottom,
fish sleep the winter wound in
filaments of ice, like mummies.
On my last night, I examine a crude map,
crayoned in blue, passed down to me

from a man dead two centuries,
whose name I carry, and whom
I am said to resemble:
it describes the coordinates of a lake,
a barren field, and the stone house
an even remoter ancestor abandoned
to come to this town.
If I were to search it out
(and circle the lake, cross the field),
where would that take me
and what shadows would I stir
and who would be there telling me
I could never escape the past?
Telling me I could never leave.